Emma Mora

MORTIMER VISITS SANTA CLAUS

Illustrations by Kennedy

Translation by Jean Grasso Fitzpatrick

BARRON'S

New York/London/Toronto/Sydney

At the top of the world, very close to the North Pole, there is a cloud called the Cloud of Golden Dreams. On this magic cloud, covered with soft snow, everything is very quiet. All you can hear are the birds singing and the jingling of the bells on Santa's sleigh. That's because this is where Santa Claus lives!

As usual in December, Santa is very busy. It's almost Christmas, and children from all over the world are sending letters to the Cloud of Golden Dreams. Santa is doing his best to make every child happy.

Santa is checking his reindeer to make sure they're ready for the long trip around the world on Christmas Eve. Every month of the year he hangs a tiny silver bell around one of his reindeer's necks. And when all twelve reindeer have bells, that means it's Christmastime!

After Christmas is over, Santa takes the tiny bells off the reindeer and hangs them on the front door of his house. That way, he can hear them ring if anyone comes to visit.

And soon, someone *will* be coming to visit.

Until this year, even though many children wrote to Santa, none of them thought of coming to see him. So the tiny bells hung on his door never jingled.

But one day in early December…

…Santa Claus was busy shining the antlers and hooves of one of his reindeer. Then he hung the last tiny silver bell around the reindeer's neck.

"That makes twelve! We're all set! Ho, ho, ho, and Merry Christmas to you!" said Santa Claus.

Then he picked up his bag of letters and went into the house. He sank into an armchair by the fireplace, put on his glasses, and read the first letter out loud:

Dear Santa,

I'm not writing to ask for toys or candy or chocolates. I'm just asking for a favor. Let me visit you for a while. That would be the best present of all, because I've decided that when I grow up I want to be Santa Claus just like you. If I could visit you, I could learn to do your job. Please make my dream come true. One day I might follow in your footsteps.

Mortimer

Santa Claus was so astonished that his glasses nearly fell off his nose. He stroked his beard thoughtfully. He had never thought of being Santa Claus as a job before, and he had certainly never imagined anyone following in his footsteps.

"Ever since there was a Christmas, *I've* always been Santa Claus. And as long as there are children, I always will be. Why do we need another Santa?" he grumbled. "Hmmf! These kids today!" He sighed and shook his head, making the pompom on his red cap bob up and down.

That night, he went to bed in a bad mood. He even forgot to eat dinner or say goodnight to his reindeer. With a big puff he blew out the little star that lit his room and pulled his red cap over his nose.

He didn't even realize that he'd gotten under the covers with his clothes and boots still on.

That night, Santa didn't sleep a wink. He thought the problem was his pillow, which was made of clouds. So he shook it a few times to make it more comfortable, but it was no use.

The real reason he couldn't fall asleep was that for the first time in his whole life, he was going to have to say "No" to a child.

He finally managed to doze off just before dawn.

That morning, two reindeer woke him up. Their job was to get the mail, because they could run as fast as the wind. As usual, there were thousands and thousands of letters.

Children with a sweet tooth asked for mountains of fudge. Lonely ones asked for a little brother or sister to play with. One child wanted a puppy, another a pony, someone a drum, someone a doll. There were others who asked for a pipe for Grandfather or a job for Daddy or a little bit of happiness.

But there was also a letter from the little boy who had made Santa Claus very, very uneasy.

At the very bottom of the sack Santa found this note:

Dear Santa, please don't forget. Come and get me—
I'm waiting for you.

Mortimer

"Here he is again, that Mortimer!" exclaimed Santa Claus, who was starting to get annoyed. "But I've already decided to tell him 'No.' Nobody can *become* Santa Claus. You have to be *born* Santa Claus—as I was. When Mortimer grows up he can be a farmer or a musician or whatever he wants, but not Santa Claus. After all, there already *is* one—me!"

But he wasn't angry for long. More than anything else, he was very sad that he had decided not to grant Mortimer's wish. Santa thought and thought. Finally, he decided that he should at least *see* this Mortimer.

So he went outside, climbed the highest fir tree and aimed his magic telescope toward the earth, right at Mortimer's house.

The house was red, with a snow-covered roof. Smoke was coming from the chimney.

With his magic telescope Santa could not only see far away and through walls, but he could also hear everything people were saying. As he looked at Mortimer's house Santa discovered that there was no mother or father.

There were five children of various ages sitting around the table. There was Penny, the eldest sister, who took care of the younger children. She was busy making dinner.

There was also a little cat who had his own seat at the table with the children!

Santa Claus saw a boy who was about eight years old, with shining hair and big eyes.

The boy was pressing his nose against a window, as though he were waiting for someone. Every so often he glanced at the baby girl who was sleeping in a cradle beside him.

"Santa Claus," he whispered, "I know you're coming, I know you're coming…"

And Santa knew that this boy was Mortimer.

The longer he watched, the more he realized that he could never refuse to grant Mortimer's wish. So he climbed down the fir tree, gathered a handful of stardust, and blew it toward the earth.

The tiny sparkles formed letters in the sky—that's how Santa Claus sends his messages. And Mortimer who was still gazing at the sky, read the shining words:

DEAR MORTIMER,
I WILL BE WAITING FOR YOU AT MIDNIGHT IN THE PINE FOREST NEAR THE SWAN LAKE. BE THERE.

SANTA CLAUS

"I certainly will!" exclaimed Mortimer, who was beside himself with joy.

But quickly the townspeople realized it was a false alarm. Christmas was seven days away. So they all went back to bed.

"Here we are!" shouted Mortimer happily. And the reindeer stopped right in front of him.

Mortimer wasn't alone.

"Welcome, Santa Claus," he said with a smile. "This is my baby sister, Betty, and here is Frisky, my cat."

"Oh, no, Mortimer," protested Santa Claus, who wasn't used to surprises. "Only *you* were supposed to come with me! I'm sorry, but they'll have to stay here."

Mortimer, Betty, and Frisky all looked at Santa very sadly. Then Mortimer explained that at his house each child had chores to do. His job was to take care of Betty and Frisky. "How can I leave them alone? They need me," he said.

Santa Claus grumbled a little. But then he said, "Well, I guess they'll have to come, too."

Mortimer let Santa hold his little sister and showed him what was inside the bundle he was carrying: Betty's bottle, a ball of yarn for Frisky to play with, his teddy bear, lumps of sugar for the reindeer, and a loaf of fresh bread to eat on the trip.

Then, with a mysterious smile, Mortimer took out a package wrapped in golden paper. "This is a present for you," he said. "I'll put it under a fir tree and you'll open it on Christmas night."

Santa looked at the package excitedly. No one had ever given *him* a present before! This is going to be a wonderful Christmas, he thought.

He was so happy that he felt like turning cartwheels in the snow, but he thought that would be undignified. So he just smiled at Betty and cuddled her.

Mortimer put Frisky and his bundle in the sleigh. Then he sat down beside Santa. "We're ready to go!" said Mortimer impatiently.

The trip to the Cloud of Golden Dreams, in the bluest part of the sky, was very exciting.

As the sleigh sped through the sky, Mortimer could reach out and touch the stars.

As soon as he stepped onto the magical white cloud, Mortimer looked around, amazed. Everything was perfectly neat and absolutely quiet!

In Santa Claus's house, there was no fire in the fireplace. There weren't any curtains on the windows, either, and the walls were bare.

Mortimer suddenly felt a little bit lonely. How different this was from his own home! They always had a blazing fire there, and you could hear the sound of children's voices.

Poor Santa Claus, thought Mortimer. Everyone asks him for presents at Christmas and then we forget all about him. He must be lonely! Mortimer threw his arms around Santa, gave him a big kiss on the cheek, and said, "Now I'm here to keep you company!"

In a few days, Santa's house began to look like a real home. A fire blazed in the fireplace. Mortimer hung pretty curtains on the windows and he painted flowers, butterflies, and a big sun on the walls.

Mortimer helped Santa make toys and candy. He kept the house neat and did all the cooking.

Santa had never been taken care of so well in his whole life, so he was in a very good mood.

The night before Christmas Eve, Mortimer told him, "Betty needs a bath. That's something only a grown-up can do—it's not easy to bathe a baby. Could you please do it?"

"Give Betty a bath? What will I have to do next?" cried Santa in dismay. But he thought for a minute and said, "I guess it won't be too hard. I'll give her a good rinse in the stream."

Mortimer looked at him in amazement. "Outside? In the ice and snow?"

"What's wrong with that?" asked Santa, puzzled. "The fish swim there all the time!"

"That's true," answered Mortimer, "but Betty isn't a fish. And if it were up to me, I'd give those poor fish little overcoats for Christmas."

"Overcoats for fish? Ho, ho, ho, that's a good one," laughed Santa. But then, seeing that Mortimer didn't think it was funny, he asked seriously, "Where do you think I should give Betty a bath?"

Mortimer suggested a tub near the warm fire.

Santa ran outside with a big bucket. He got water from the stream and filled the tub. Then he picked up Betty and put her in.

As soon as Betty's foot touched the icy water, she let out a wail and clung to Santa's beard for dear life.

Frisky was so scared he hid under the couch.

"What's wrong?" asked Mortimer.

"She won't take a bath, the naughty girl," replied Santa Claus.

"That's funny," said Mortimer. "Usually she loves to splash in the water." He stuck his hand into the tub and quickly pulled it out. "This water is ice cold!" he cried. "You have to heat it."

So Santa heated it on the fire and then put Betty back in the tub.

Betty let Santa wash her. She had a great time getting soap and water all over the place.

By the time the bath was over, Santa even had soap suds on his nose and on his red suit, but he had never had so much fun.

He dried Betty carefully, dusted her with baby powder, dressed her, and combed her hair.

Later on, he lay the baby down in her crib and sang a lullaby that he made up as he went along:

Sleep, baby, sleep,
The stars shine bright,
Christmas Eve's tomorrow night.
Sleep, baby, sleep,
On this magic cloud above,
Dream of peace and joy and love.

After she fell asleep, Santa softly kissed Betty's cheek and murmured, "How happy it would make me to be your father…"

Mortimer gave him a hug and whispered, "You'd be a wonderful father."

It was almost Christmas Eve. Night was falling. Mortimer took Santa's hand and led him to the fir tree where he had put his present. When Santa unwrapped it, he was delighted to find just what he had always wanted: a beautiful buckle for his belt and a pair of cozy slippers.

"They belonged to my Dad," Mortimer explained. "He's gone now, and I'd like you to have them."

"I have something for you, too, and for Betty and Frisky," said Santa. He pulled the three brightest stars from the sky—one for each child, and one for the cat— and hung them on golden chains around their necks. "These stars hold all my love for you."

He also gave Mortimer a magic telescope like his own and said, "Tonight you will help me bring presents to all the children of the world. Then I will take you home so that you can spend Christmas with Penny and your family. I know you'll miss me, but anytime you want to see me, just look up through this telescope at my cloud."

At dawn, Santa Claus returned from his trip around the world. He came into the house, but suddenly it seemed too big and empty. He was happy to see that Mortimer had set out breakfast on the table. Then he noticed a card sticking out from under the plate.

He read it in a wink:

Dear Father (You'll let me call you that, won't you?),
    Betty, Frisky and I have been very happy with you. We'll come back soon. We love you very much.

Hugs and kisses,
Mortimer

Santa Claus realized that his eyes were filled with tears. But they were tears of happiness, so he didn't bother drying them. Now he had a little boy, a little girl, and a cat! And they'd all be back!

He saw Mortimer's teddy bear on the bed, Betty's bottle on the table, and Frisky's ball of yarn on the floor, near the fireplace. They *would* be back—he was sure of it. And he didn't feel lonely anymore.

So, if someday you meet a boy and a girl with stars shining around their necks, you'll know that they're Mortimer and Betty—Santa Claus's children. And if you see a little cat, with the same star around its neck, that's Frisky, Santa Claus's very own cat.